This igloo book belongs to:

....

igloobooks

Published in 2022
First published in the UK by Igloo Books Ltd
An imprint of Igloo Books Ltd
Cottage Farm, NN6 0BJ, UK
Owned by Bonnier Books
Sveavägen 56, Stockholm, Sweden
www.igloobooks.com

0522 004
4 6 8 10 11 9 7 5
ISBN 978-1-80022-675-3

Written by Sienna Williams
Illustrated by Benedetta Capriotti

Designed by Jason Shortland
Edited by James Phoenix

Printed and manufactured in China

ONE MILLION
Kisses

igloobooks

Colourful. **Sweet.**
A **sticky**, fun treat.

Like ice cream with
ZILLIONS of sprinkles on top,
I love you **SO MUCH** and
I will never stop.

Yucky and green. Eat them and I'll **scream!**

Like **HUNDREDS** of peas left in piles on my plate,
my love feels **ENDLESS** and I think you're great.

Pop! in the air.
Rainbow swirls everywhere.

Like **THOUSANDS** of bubbles we blow by the lake,
I love you **MORE** with each breath that I take.

Some **big**. Others *small*.
They creep and they crawl.

Like **BILLIONS** of bugs
that all flutter and buzz,
our love is **UNIQUE.**
No one else is like us.

Pew, what a smell.
So **whiffy** as well!

Like **DOZENS** of
dirty socks lost on my floor,
my love keeps on **GROWING**
like never before.

Shiny and **bright**.
Pink, purple and white.

Like **TEN THOUSAND** shells that wash up by the sea, our love is **FOREVER** and was meant to be.

Like **HEAPS** of toy cars in the race game we play,
I love that we **ALWAYS** have fun every day.

Soft, **cuddly** fun.

Best friends,
every one.

Like **TOO MANY** teddies I can't even count,
I'll always love you a **GIANT** amount!

Tens, hundreds, thousands and **MILLIONS**, too.
Sprinkles on ice cream. How much I love...

... **YOU!**